S0-AFV-356

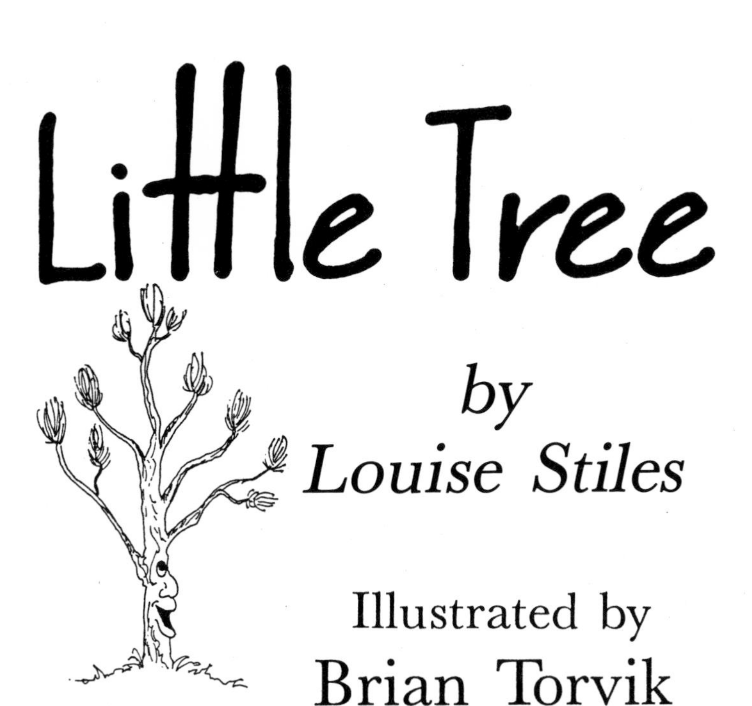

Little Tree

by
Louise Stiles

Illustrated by
Brian Torvik

GRANNY STILES MINISTRIES
Clewiston, Florida

Dedication

This book is dedicated to my Lord,
to whom all credit is due.

Louise Stiles

Little Tree
ISBN 0-88144-051-5 AP-051-795

P. O. Box 1656
Clewiston, FL 33440

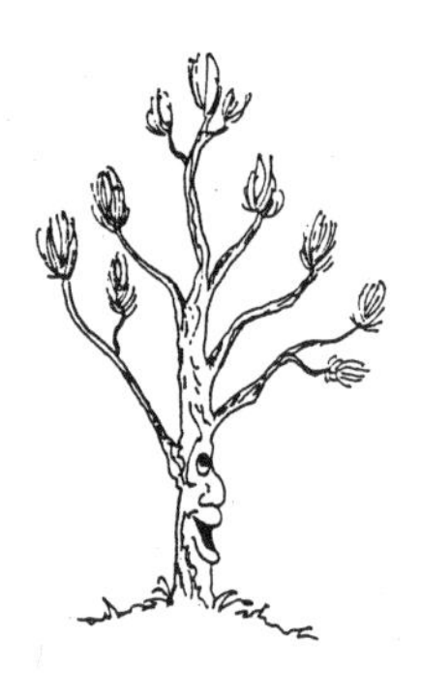

Published by Granny Stiles Ministries
P.O. Box 1656
Clewiston, FL 33440

Manufactured by Lake Book Manufacturing
Melrose Park, IL

Printed in the United States of America.

TO: Wesley Billing

FROM: Great Grandma Robinson

DATE: 10-16-1993

And Jesus prayed this prayer: "O Father, Lord of heaven and earth, thank you for hiding the truth from those who think themselves so wise, and for revealing it to little children. Yes, Father, for it pleased you to do it this way! . . ."

Matthew 11:25,26
TLB

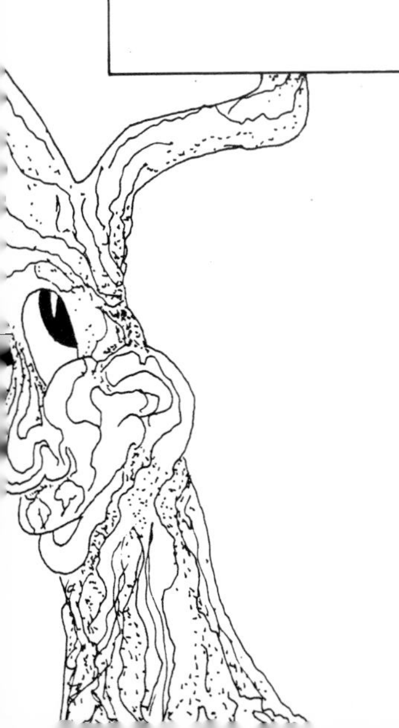

Little Tree

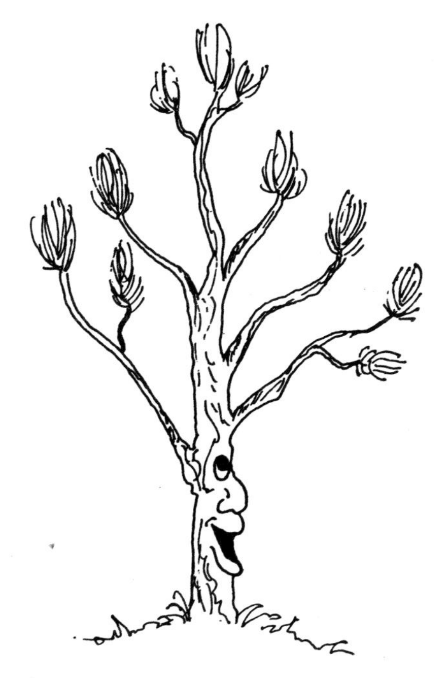

In December of 1983, outside a little town called Clewiston, Florida, a group of trees were talking. Big Tree said to the others, "It's almost time for us to celebrate Jesus' birthday."

Little Tree said, "Who is Jesus?"

"Boy, you mean to tell me you don't know that Jesus is God's Son?" Big Tree replied.

"Who is God?" asked Little Tree.

"Well," said Big Tree, "I guess this time last year you weren't any bigger than a switch, so it is about time you got educated. Boy, do you see that sun up there in the sky? God made that sun to keep you warm and make you grow."

In amazement Little Tree said, "I didn't know that." "Well, that's right," Big Tree explained, "you know the rain that falls so you can have a cool drink of water? Well, God made the rain."

"And you see that little sparrow on your branch? Well, God made that little bird."

Little Tree laughed and said, "I like that little bird. He tickles me when he walks on me."

"Well, Little Tree," Big Tree exclaimed, "God made that bird, and all our friends in the woods. In fact, God made you and me and everything in the whole wide world. God looked at everything that He had made and said, 'This is good.'

"Then, Little Tree, God made man and woman in His own image and blessed them. He brought every living thing He had made to man and told him to name everything and to rule over them. He told man and woman to enjoy all of the fruit trees except the tree of the knowledge of good and evil. God told them to leave that fruit alone for if they ate it they would surely die.

"Oh, how God loved man that He had made. In the cool of the day God would visit with them in the garden. But one day, Little Tree, man and woman disobeyed God and ate the fruit of the tree of knowledge, and sin came into the world and it separated man from God. It broke God's heart because He could not have fellowship with man whom He loved so much.

"And it came to pass, God's Son, Jesus, asked His Father if it was time for Him to go to earth and die for the sins of man.

"God said, 'It is hard for Me to let You go! You are My only Son!'

"Jesus said, 'Father, I delight to do Thy will.' "

"By a miracle, Little Tree, Jesus was born to a virgin named Mary, way . . . way . . . far in the east, in a little town called Bethlehem," Big Tree continued.

In wonderment, Little Tree said, "Nobody ever told me that."

"Well, that's right, boy," replied Big Tree. "Jesus grew up and when He became a man He suffered many things and died on the cross for the sins of the people. But Jesus did not stay dead. He arose from the dead and went back to Heaven with God His Father.

"And that's the reason we celebrate Christmas," Big Tree concluded.

Little Tree, with much excitement, said, "I never heard such a good story!"

"That's right," said Big Tree, "this story has been told for nearly 2,000 years."

In deep thought, Little Tree said, "I wish I had something to give to Jesus for His birthday."

Big Tree said, "Boy, you don't have anything to give to Jesus. Just look at ya; you hardly have any leaves on your branches. I wasn't gonna tell you this, boy, but you're downright ugly! I'm talking ug...ly!"

God, I love You

But you know, boys and girls, that night after all Little Tree's friends were asleep, he lifted up his branches and very simply said, "God, I love You for making me, and I love Your Son, Jesus. I wish I had something to give Him for His birthday."

He rested his branches and fell asleep.

Bright and early the next morning, Grandpa Stiles was in the same area as Big Tree and Little Tree. He looked at the tall trees with their beautiful leaves and was about to leave when he spied Little Tree. He walked back to his truck, took out his saw and began cutting down Little Tree.

Little Tree woke up startled and in pain. He began to cry, "Please, Mister, stop. You're hurting me! Please, Mister, stop. You're hurting me!"

About that time, Grandpa stopped. Stepping back, he wiped his brow and spoke aloud, "Grandma said she had to have a very special tree for children's church to celebrate Jesus' birthday, and I think this little fellow will be just fine."

Little Tree began to cry even harder, but this time for joy, because God had answered his prayer.

Big Tree called to all their friends of the woods and shouted, "Did you hear that? They're going to use Little Tree for Jesus' birthday!"

All of Little Tree's friends began to dance and clap their branches.

Grandpa took Little Tree to the church where Grandma was waiting with a basket of decorations. Together they put Little Tree on a stand. Then upon his branches, Grandma placed beautiful lights, for Jesus is truly the Light of the World. At the top of Little Tree's branches she placed a star, for it was a star that led the wise men to Bethlehem where Jesus was born.

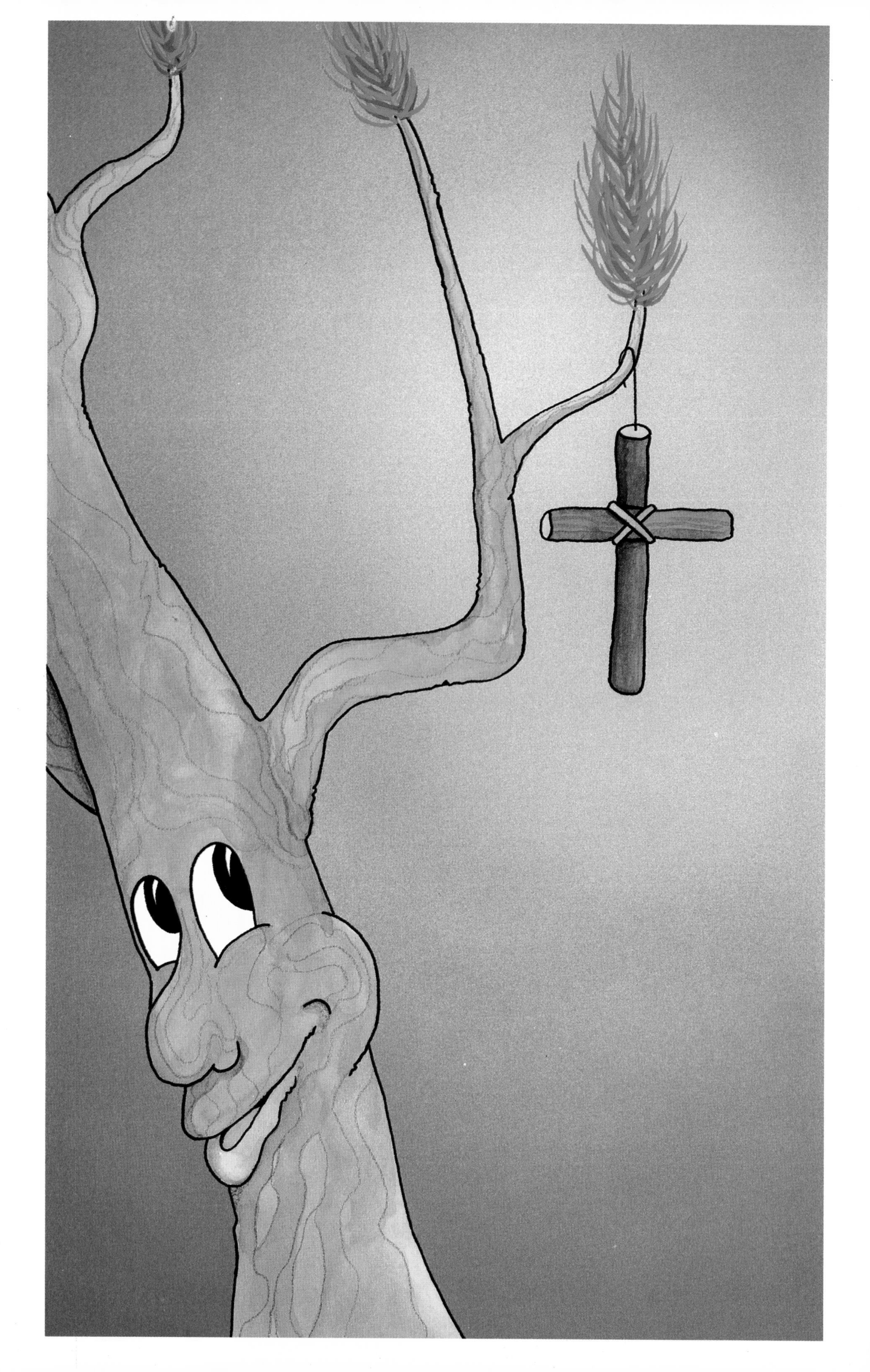

Then ever so carefully upon a branch a cross was placed, for it was upon the cross that Jesus shed His blood for the people. Without the shedding of Jesus' blood, there would be no forgiveness for our sins.

An Easter lily was the next ornament placed on Little Tree. It speaks to us of life. Jesus did not stay in the grave; He arose from the dead.

For God so loved the world, that he gave his only begotten Son, that whosoever believeth in him should not perish, but have everlasting life (John 3:16).

Last, but not least, tucked far back in the corner of Grandma's basket was a "You Are Special" snowflake. Lovingly, she placed it on one of Little Tree's branches. Though billions of snowflakes have fallen, there are no two alike. Even though God has made many people, they are likened to *the stars of the heaven, and . . . the sand which is upon the sea shore* (Gen. 22:17). They cannot be numbered. God made only one exactly like you.

So, remember little people, red or yello[w] black or white, you are precious in His sigh[t].

Like Little Tree, God loves YOU — You are Special!

And so it was on Christmas Eve night that Little Tree was happier than he had ever been before, and it was all because he had given himself to Jesus.

Little Tree

I'm little tree and I once lived in the woods,
with trees so big and so tall —
why, they just made me feel,
like I was nothing at all.

Then, I heard about Jesus,
and how He was born on Christmas Day;
about how He lived and died for all people,
for their sins He did gladly pay.

So, I opened my heart to Jesus.
I said, "I wish I had something to give You,"
and before I knew what was happening,
He said, "But, Little Tree, you do!"

You see, when we're willing to give of ourselves,
and we give Him our very best —
then He will come in and be with us;
and He will take care of the rest.

He made us each one different,
but we're all special, that's true;
we are precious in His sight,
'cause He loves me and you.

So, let us celebrate His birthday,
and share the joy that He will give,
not only just on Christmas Day —
but each day that we live.

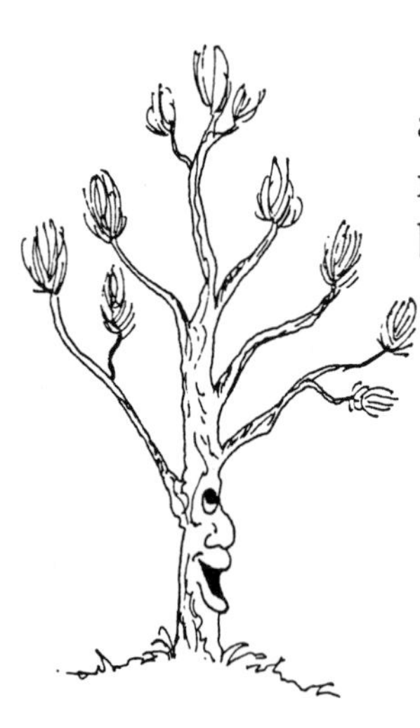

Author, Donna Wiggins

About the Author

The author was born Nellie Louise Hoffman on July 2, 1935, on Market Street in Memphis, Tennessee. She is the mother of five children — one boy and four girls — and the grandmother of eight.

Before she was born, her mother gave her to the Lord. Her testimony is that she cannot remember a moment in which God wasn't a part of her life.

In 1954 she totally consecrated her life to the Lord Jesus Christ and received the Holy Spirit. It was at that time that God asked if she would teach His Word. Her reply was that she didn't know how, that she needed someone to teach her. The Lord told her that if she would be willing, He would help her. To this she responded, "Yes, Lord, take my life and use it for Your glory." Louise has been in children's work since that time. She has taught Sunday School and children's church.

As a result of a tragic hunting accident in 1987, her wonderful husband, Gilbert was suddenly taken home to be with the Lord.

God has been very faithful to her through this, and many storms of life.

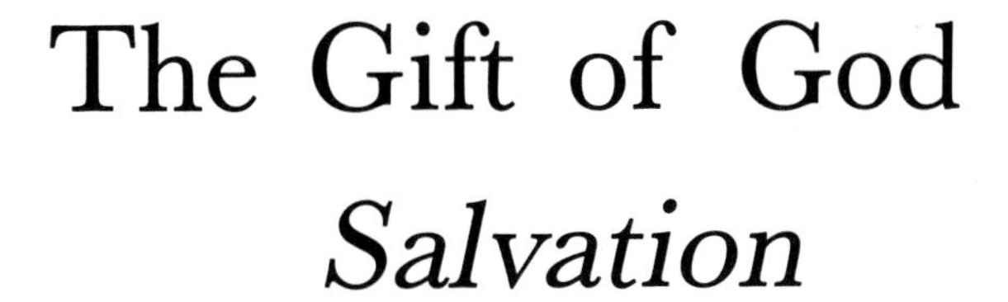

The Gift of God

Salvation

Dear Jesus, thank You for Little Tree.

I thank You for loving me and making

me special!

I receive Your gift of Everlasting Life.

Come, live in me, Jesus!

Amen

Signed ______________________________

Date __________

The book you have just read was inspired by the Holy Spirit. My latest book *"Sir Lovealot"* will be published soon. I would be pleased to hear from you. I can be contacted at this address:

GRANNY STILES MINISTRIES

P. O. BOX 1656

CLEWISTON, FL 33440

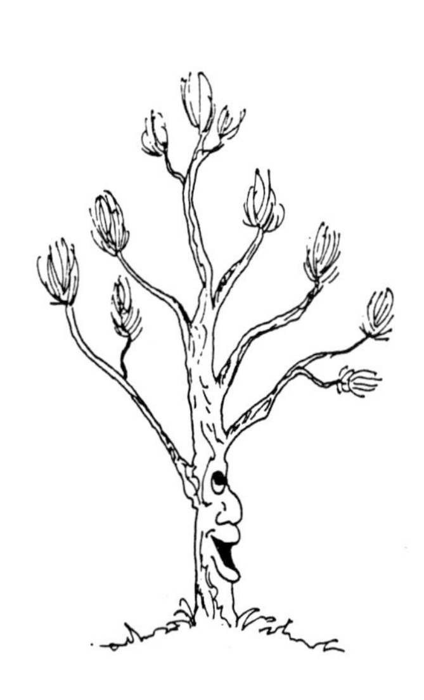